The Sapphire Chronicles
Broken Lair

E. Hughes

Love-LovePublishing, Madison, WI
Paperback Edition: 978-1-961823-18-1
eBook ISBN: 978-1-7377052-7-7
Title: *The Sapphire Chronicles, Broken Lair*
E. Hughes

Second Edition
First edition, 2012

From the Earth sprouted the strangest of loves

Other novels and works by E. Hughes:

Fiction:

Sixth Iteration
Disappear, Love
Business as Usual
Infatuation
A Mediterranean Romance: The Capa Royals
The Sapphire Chronicles: Broken Lair
Hello (A Screenplay)
Beyond the Plain (Poetry)
Digital Smiles (Poetry)

Children's Books:

Penelope Helps Mom and Dad
Penelope: Be Kind to Animals
Penelope: Super Duper Spectacular Princess Ballerina
Penelope: Don't be afraid
Penelope Holiday Cheer
Garden of Secrets

Nonfiction

Time and the Multi-Universe: A philosophy of time and time travel
Starting Your First Patio Garden: A Coffee Book
Family in a Time of Covid-19: The Truth about Coronavirus, How to Protect Yourself and Prepare
Reality Unbound (2024)

Chapter 1

Sapphire

It was hard to look away from her perky bright eyes. They drew him in, seduced him…until common sense leaked out of his head like there was a gaping hole in it. Sapphire peeked at him from the corner of her book and grinned like she'd hidden a pearl underneath her silky tongue. She was reading Molière… sophisticated thing that she was. He watched her lips move as she read each word in French, her lips forming a perfect pout. He thought, he ought not to be staring at this stunningly beautiful woman. He, an old married man and father of a three year-old big headed son.

Harrison Brooks had gone out that day in pursuit of peace and quiet yet he had found anything but. Instead he'd found this jewel, this precious, darling woman, who'd possessed the yearnings of his body and mind like a spirit haunting an old house. He would have said something to her—if not for the book in her hand. Manners dictated that he not interrupt… especially when the view was damned better from where he sat. The only thing he couldn't see was her legs. *'Get up,'* he thought. *'Get out of your seat so I can peek at that sexy ass of yours…'* No. Much too vulgar for a man like Harrison. But something in her brought out the animal in him. He mentally growled as he imagined Sapphire with her clothes off. What was he thinking? Was he really *that* lonely?

Sapphire tried to keep her eyes on her book. But it was distracting. The staring…she had even looked over at him and smirked, an invitation for him to say something, if he had something to say.

Sapphire was used to being watched and leered at by strange men, but *this* was disconcerting. Perhaps, because they were alone in the most deserted quarter of the city's downtown library in an area where the lights dimmed—after fifteen minutes of inactivity. She'd made a habit of reading there because she liked the seclusion, the damp musty smell of books, and darkness. But the stranger was invading her space. Her private sanctuary since her breakup with Victor Reid, the only man she ever loved. Victor had promised her the world and she betrayed him, creating a powerful enemy in the process. A man so dangerous, Sapphire was forced to live off the grid. And yet, she still loved him. She often wondered what life would be like had she not betrayed him. But he was a bad man. A dangerous man. Sapphire quieted the nagging regretful voice at the back of her mind—she'd done the right thing.

She dated from time to time, hoping someone new would replace him in her heart. But none did. None could. And none would…*ever*. Most guys were skeptical of her observing, secretive nature…qualities she'd found difficult to fix, even in her spare time. She'd been unemployed for a while though, and hoped her "old way" of doing things would eventually abate as she tried to assume a normal life…or at least, as normal as her present occupation as a former spy turned private detective allowed.

After Sapphire's eyes connected a few times more with the stranger, she finally decided it was time to go. *Would he follow her?*

She left her seat at the table and placed her book back on the shelf. Librarians hated that— when borrowers put their own books away. They suggested leaving them on the table for the clerks to restock. But Sapphire wanted the area to appear undisturbed so that no one except

Mrs. Chapman, the head librarian, bothered to check in but a few times a week.

Sapphire reluctantly put Molière back in its place—on the bottom shelf. But as she bent over she felt the heat of Harrison's gaze upon her back. She turned and grimaced. The traces of an impish smile appeared on his lips as Sapphire followed his line of view directly to her perfectly shaped ass. He looked up, boldly meeting her eyes, the expression on his ruggedly handsome face apologetic.

"Sorry," he said, rising from his chair. "I couldn't help but notice your skirt. Is that from the Givenchy spring line? I'm a huge fan of his designs."

What kind of dumb ass excuse was that? she thought, narrowing her eyes contemptuously.

"Why? Are you in the fashion industry?"

Sapphire offered him her steeliest gaze. No need to be friendly to the man. There were at least ten tables—all of them unoccupied, and he had to sit at hers. What a fool. The area of the library they were in was four levels underground, basement levels. Few people were interested in the obscure French poetry and the literature she read. Especially people who lived in fast-paced urbane cities like New York.

"Not exactly. I'm Harrison Brooks, nice to meet you," he said, offering a hand. "And you are?"

Sapphire reluctantly accepted his handshake. Harrison took her hand within his and seductively caressed the back of her hand with his thumb. Her skin was soft, just as he'd imagined it. He could smell the sweet scent of jasmine soap on her skin.

"I'm Sapphire," she replied, crossly meeting his gaze as she drew her fingers away.

"Sapphire? That's an interesting name."

"So I hear," she quipped.

"Do you have a last name?" Harrison smirked, displaying a mouth full of perfect teeth.

His eyes looked too round—like a pair of pots staring back at her. Yet his smile was so infectious, Sapphire couldn't help but smile back—but only for a second. She wasn't in the habit of smiling. He seemed harmless enough... and he was handsome enough too. He was tall, dark, broad-shouldered, with dark-hair, dressed casually in a white t-shirt, jeans, and the black European-styled jacket that he'd left draped over the back of his chair.

"Just Sapphire," she answered, pinching her soft pink lips into a frown.

She knew what he was thinking. She could see it in his eyes. She didn't know why it bothered her, but it did. He thinks she's a stripper, albeit a very pretty one. But Harrison knew better. How many strippers had time to read Molière or any other obscure French literature in an isolated section of a public library? Perhaps he was stereotyping. Maybe exotic dancers did in fact, have time to read obscure French literature, so what did he know? But Sapphire was refined and elegant unlike the scantily attired women who danced onstage in seedy bars before hoards of horny leering men at night. This was no stripper. She was sexy even with all of her clothes on. Less was definitely more, and Harrison wanted to see what Sapphire hid underneath the ruffled collar of the cream-colored chiffon blouse she wore. Maybe it was the intimacy of being alone that aroused him so. He didn't know what had come over him, but he wanted her and felt the heat of his desire rising in his pants.

"My father named me Sapphire, actually," she self-consciously offered.

"That's an odd name for a pretty brown-eyed girl."

"He didn't name me Sapphire because of my eye color, not that it's any of your business."

"Fair enough. Though, if you don't mind my saying, your eyes are absolutely breathtaking. Alluring...they're mesmerizing.

She gave him a skeptical look. Sapphire had always made an effort to blend in and to stand out only when she needed to. She was definitely okay with dark brown eyes. It was the most common eye color on the planet, so what was he going on about?

"Sorry—but I'm not impressed by cheap pick lines. So I don't even think—"

"I'm just trying to pay you a compliment."

"What exactly do you find so alluring about my eyes? I use them to see. I got two of 'em, just like everybody else." She flipped through the pages of another book.

"Just like everybody else, huh? You have no idea what gorgeous pair of eyes like yours do to a man. I damn near melted in my seat looking into those coal black almond shaped eyes of yours."

Harrison found Sapphire's dark exotic eyes, raven black hair, and deep mocha complexion sexy as hell. To Harrison, she looked like a very passionate woman...all buttoned up in pretty clothes just longing for someone to rip them off… and he was more than capable of doing the job.

"If what I saw in your eyes was like anyone else's, I wouldn't be talking to you."

He was coming on strong. "And what exactly do you see?" she challenged.

"A very beautiful liar."

Sapphire bristled at his words. Who in the hell was he to call her a liar or talk to her like he actually knew anything about her life? She was in the business of lying, but considered herself to be anything but a liar, at least—off the clock. Lying was part of the job. Nothing more.

"And you know all of this about me in the span of a few minutes?"

"I see a woman pretending to be something she's not. You're not as tough as you want people think. You're quite fragile, actually. I find it endearing."

"Why, because it makes you feel like a big strong man?" The last thing anyone who actually knew her, would call her, is *fragile*. The man was living in a fantasy world.

"Because you're the type of woman who deserves to be loved…*but* you're wary, afraid of being hurt."

"I'm afraid of being annoyed," Sapphire shot back.

Harrison smiled.

"What I don't understand is why a beautiful woman like you would choose to hide all the way down here in the basement? You're punishing the entire world by depriving it of your breathtaking beauty. You deserve to be out in sunshine, the moonlight, or better yet, in my arms."

She hid in the basement because she was on the run. If Victor found her... there's no telling what he would do.

"Maybe I want to be alone. Ever think about that?"

"*That*...would be a crime against humanity," Harrison smiled.

Sapphire rolled her eyes. Harrison was really starting to get on her nerves. He was way too forward.

"Am I supposed to take this as a *compliment*? Spare me the cheesy lines, okay? I'm not here for that."

"You can take it however you want," Harrison answered. "What do you do for a living?"

"I live for a living, how about you?

"I meet beautiful women. I fall for them occasionally."

"Occupational Hazard?"

"Sometimes. Depends on the woman. I'm an aviation executive at Brook Engineering. That is,

I build and sell aviation parts to companies, actually."

"Am I supposed to be impressed?"

"Most people are."

"I'm not most people," Sapphire replied.

She had a talent for seeing through bullshit and he was full of it. Harrison sat in his chair, slid the wedding band he wore off of his finger and tucked it into his front pocket.

"Duly noted..." he answered.

" —Good. I have to go. It was a pleasure,"

"Why?"

"Stimulating as it is, the library is hardly the place for conversation," she answered.

"Can I take you somewhere?"

"For what?"

"To talk…"

"I came here to get away from that."

"Get away from what?"

"People."

"I'm not most people," Harrison retorted, flinging her words right back at her.

"It's late and I'm hungry. Good night."

Sapphire started towards the exit. He had to say something, *do* something before she slipped away. Harrison knew the late-night hour was just an excuse to get rid of him. It was only seven o' clock. The library closed at eleven.

"Late for what?" he asked, refusing to be dismissed.

"Dinner. *Life.* Some of us have those, you know..."

"What if I bought dinner?"

"I can buy my own food."

"I know—but..."

Harrison jumped out of his chair and slipped into his jacket.

"Don't go anywhere," he ordered, shrugging his arms through the straps of his backpack.

"I can't make any promises," she answered, raising her hands defensively.

"I know."

"Then why on earth should I wait for *you*?"

"Because you're curious," he grinned.

"Curious about what?"

"Me," he grinned.

Cocky bastard...

He was right. But only *half*-right. She was curious and only stayed long enough to hear him out...so why not stay a little longer? Besides, it was too late to hide from him anyway. It wasn't like she had anything better to do…just an empty studio in a cramped apartment building to go home to.

Sapphire watched as Harrison zigzagged through the aisles and made a beeline to the nearest exit. He was nice enough, but he'd all but taken over her special place…ruining the tranquility with his lustful presence. But is that not what she wanted? Someone to disturb her tranquility? Harrison wasn't hard on the eyes either. For a slim man, his arms, chest, and torso were ripped with muscles in all the right places. She liked that.

Sapphire grabbed a book, sat down, and idly flipped through the pages. She'd give him five minutes. No—ten, and then she was out of there. But as much as she wanted to read she couldn't concentrate on the words, much less translate them. Victor suggested she learn French to not only occupy her time, but to avail herself to French ballet directors. Sapphire was a good dancer, not a *great* one. An injury early in her career had seen to that so his faith had been entirely misplaced. She would never recover her ability to dance or her ballet career again. At the time, Victor was working on something big, bigger than she could have ever imagined. They broke up because of a "conflict" with his work. That was a long time ago, but she still found Victor hard to get over because of the abrupt, dramatic conclusion of their relationship. Maybe Harrison was just the distraction she needed to forget the man she'd spent the past eighteen months longing for.

Harrison returned ten minutes later, his hair damp from the rain. Water dripped from his black European-styled jacket to the floor, his white t-shirt clinging to his muscular chest.

"You're still here," he smirked.

Indeed. Not even Sapphire expected to go on an impromptu date. He wanted to play a game, so she was going to play it with him. What the hell—she was bored out of her mind anyway.

"So I am."

The backpack Harrison wore had been slung carefully over one of his arms, and it was full of contraband. She could smell it all the way from her seat.

"I knew you would be."

"Do I hear gloating?" Sapphire shot back, shooting him a warning look. "That could change, you know."

"Namaste," Harrison said, bowing his head apologetically. "I don't mean to be—arrogant. I'm just happy you're here."

"Thank you," Sapphire smiled. "I appreciate your *heartfelt* confession," she added sarcastically.

Harrison opened his backpack and dumped the contents onto the table. Four cartons of takeout from the Chinese restaurant across the street and a pair of candles. Sapphire was familiar with the restaurant. She'd eaten there numerous times. It was one of her favorite places.

"Pick your poison... noodles, fried rice. General Tsao Chicken, and cookies for dessert."

"You can't eat that in here."

"Why not?"

"Because we're in a library. What if they catch us?"

"They'll ask us to leave," Harrison shrugged.

"Fair enough."

Sapphire grabbed a carton of noodles and a plastic fork.

"No plates?"

"We can eat straight out of the carton," He answered.

"You got this all figured out, don't you?"

"I *wish*," he said.

Harrison stuck his plastic spoon into a carton of fried rice and started to eat. They ate in silence for a while, until he looked up again, and noticed her staring at him.

"What is it?" he asked her irritably.

"Sorry," Sapphire shrugged. "But...how old are you?"

"Doesn't matter. I'm an old man now."

"You don't look old."

"I feel old."

"You're fishing for compliments."

"You got me!" he said, raising his hands in mock surrender. "I'm forty-three."

"Forty-three?" Sapphire gasped. "Is that what old passes for these days? I must be ancient in female years."

"Oh...? How old are you? You can't be any older than twenty-eight."

"I'm thirty-two."

"Thirty two year-old free spirit?"

"I'm not just a free spirit, I do have a job."

"Doing what?" Harrison asked, spooning another mountain of rice into his mouth

"As an over-the-hill ballerina," Sapphire pouted.

"Over the hill?"

"You can dance for only so long before it takes a toll on your body."

"Hmm... you're body looks fine to me!" He wiggled his eyebrows.

"That's what they all say, until they see my knee."

"What happened?"

"Nasty career-ending injury."

"I'm sorry to hear that," Harrison said.

"It's not as bad as it sounds…even though I'll never become a prima ballerina. I still dance, but I've since taken on a part-time job that has proven more interesting to me."

"Doing what?"

"How'd you get into the aviation business?" Sapphire interrupted, quickly shoveling a forkful of noodles into her mouth. The less he knew about her situation the better.

Harrison opened a can of soda and passed it to her.

"My father. You like to travel?"

"Have tickets, I'm there."

The glow of light emanating between them was intimate.

"My kind of girl," Harrison replied, a big grin on his face. His wife avoided travel at all costs, which made for an extremely boring life, stateside. But then, the woman for reasons unknown, was more than happy to send him on his way. *Alone….*

They met in college. Jane was a hard-partying sorority girl and Harrison, a dorky engineering student focused on living up to his father's expectations. He lived vicariously through her at the time. He loved her zest for life, stories about her raunchy nights out with the girls, and the occasional excitement of taking her home after a party and screwing her senseless. Jane had a reputation, but Harrison didn't mind. Academia was his first priority. He wanted a woman who was ready, easy and available after a long hard night of studying, and Jane was more than willing to oblige, requiring little by way of commitment or affection. They continued to date after graduation, and she was fun for a while. Jane had her own life, friends and interests, but things changed after they married. Harrison wished he'd taken the time to meet other women before proposing to Jane, and he resented her for it. The passion was gone from the relationship. He knew Jane wasn't the right woman for him. She wasn't his friend, companion, *or* lover. She was his partner…someone who managed Harrison's day to day life, cooking, cleaning, organizing and doing his laundry. He married her because it was the easiest thing to do at a time in his life when he was far too busy to explore other options. His world, was dull and uninteresting until he laid eyes on Sapphire, an attractive, cultured, independent, young woman. Was it a mid-life crisis that made him want to trade his wife in for a younger model? He didn't know or care. Harrison wanted Sapphire in his bed, and meant to have her.

He reached across the table and took her hand in his, his eyes smoldering with lust, hers, a mixture of trepidation and surprise.

"What are you doing?" she asked, noodles dangling out her mouth. She slurped them in and rose to her feet.

Harrison imagined her slurping *him* into her mouth. He slid out of his chair and glided towards her. He felt like an old horn dog, but didn't care. He felt connected to Sapphire, and committed himself to having her.

He took her hand within is.

"I don't like this," she said, her lips tightening into a frown.

"You don't like what?" he asked.

He looked down at her hand, small and warm within his.

"I don't like what you're doing," she answered softly, blinking sultry eyes that made his blood hot.

He slid behind her. She could feel the bulge in his pants pressing against her backside as his fingers traced up and down her arm, generating chill bumps and heat simultaneously.

Sapphire spun around so that she faced him, her back to the table now. She tried not to let her nerves get the better of her. She'd been in similar scrapes with handsome men before.

"It's late," Harrison said, feeling himself in more danger than she. "Can I walk you home?"

The dread she felt drained from her body, leaving her pale as a ghost.

"Thanks, but… I know the way," she panted. If ever there was a night not to mix business with pleasure, this was it. But it had been so long since she'd been held like this, she felt primal. He read the need in her eyes…could smell the pheromones, rising between them like a cloud of smoke, two very lonely people in a slow-moving collision.

Harrison nodded then, his fingers gripping her upper arms, almost crushing her, and she wished he'd let her go.

"Then can I have a kiss?" he asked.

Sapphire shook her head.

"That was rhetorical," Harrison smiled.

Her eyes blazing, her body, feverish, she pleaded with him to end this before they went too far…although, it wasn't as if she had no say in the matter—just that she was already too far gone. Sex was on the brain and like a runaway train, there was no stopping it. How long had it been, since she'd been with someone? Eighteen months? Longer? She deserved this…*needed this*. Harrison's breath was warm against her mouth as he drew near, and hotter still, as his lips pressed onto hers.

Sapphire arched her back as he filled his hand with the softness of her breasts through her thin chiffon blouse, her body moving in tandem with his. It was almost instinctive, the way her legs parted, so that he brushed against her, groin to groin, hand cupping her backside, drawing her onto the edge of the table. He slid his hands under her skirt and slowly, rolled her panties down to her ankles, before stripping them away and tossing them somewhere on the floor. Sapphire heard an intake of breath as she unbuckled Harrison's pants. He leaned back, allowing her space as reached into his briefs and massaged his sizeable length until he damn near came in her hand.

This is what she did. She seduced. And she was damned good at it. So good at it, even she was confused about who seduced who. She'd made a career of looking for weaknesses and exploiting them. Harrison, like all men, was at their most vulnerable in the presence of beautiful women…especially when they were lonely. Needy, middle-aged men aching for appreciation and attention was her specialty…as well as the companies they owned or worked for.

Sapphire moaned and he loved that. Harrison loved feeling desired, he loved feeling wanted, and he loved *her*… for the moment. The rhythm of their bodies vacillated from slow and steady to hard and frenzied, until he felt ready to explode. He tasted her beautiful lips again, pressing his mouth onto hers. His body trembled as Sapphire succumbed to this need and the kiss deepened. She felt—soft in his calloused grip, pliant in his forceful arms as he pressed her back against the wood table. She winced, her fingers digging into his flesh. Ravenous primitive need overtook her as she rode waves of pleasure until her thighs trembled. He touched her cheek, turning her face to his.

"Are you okay?" Harrison asked. The tips of his fingers lingered on her luminous face. He held her gaze and her heart skipped a beat.

Sapphire answered this question with a nod but closed her eyes, shutting him out as she gripped his ass and scooted forward, her hips rising to meet him more completely. His body shivered with need, his ravaged breathing filling her ears with grunting and lovemaking noises. Soon, their bodies lay tangled on top of the library table, their noses touching. Their eyes closed. Harrison stayed there, not wanting to leave, stroking her inner thigh.

Her breath was warm against his lips, coming out in small puffs. He was dreading it, leaving her. Or her leaving him. And not just because of the way he reacted to her physically. Harrison felt tiny convulsions between her quivering thighs. How in the hell was he still hard after that? The things this woman did to him…He flipped her over, his hands cupping her breasts as he bent her over the edge of the table.

Sapphire blinked. The entire room was a blur, books and all. "What have we done?" she groaned. Or worse, what if someone were to walk in and find them—Harrison with his pants down to his ankles and she, with her skirt lifted.

But Harrison couldn't let go, not now. He leaned down, turning her towards him as his mouth captured one of her breasts. He was fired up and ready to go another round. He needed only a few minutes, if she would have him. He reached down, stroking, building himself up to the mood.

"It was good, wasn't it? Let's not play that game. Don't act like you didn't want it too."

That—was a moment. A moment of anger at having sensed that what he felt for her wasn't mutual. Sapphire's hand came down on Harrison's head—hard. He winced as he drew back, a stunned look on his face. "

I'm sorry, I didn't mean it—not like that," he stammered, moving away…

"You have a knack for saying and doing things you don't mean, don't you?"

Sapphire shook her head. The musty smell of books was gone now, the stench of their lovemaking lingering in the air. She searched, scanned the room for her underwear, and found them on one of the shelves. As she bent down to gather them, a tiny metal object fell to the floor from Harrison's pocket.

His wedding ring had rolled out of his turned down pants, across the floor. Sapphire stared at it, unblinkingly for several moments, then picked it up and handed it to him.

"I can explain," Harrison started, pulling his pants up.

Yeah. She was good at this. She was the seducer, right?

"It's over between us—I swear, Jane and I…we're finished, we have been, for a long time now."

"Of course you are," Sapphire replied, a saccharine sweet smile plastered on her face.

She slid into her underwear.

"Don't leave."

Sapphire adjusted her clothes.

"Can I walk or drive you home? Can I do something?" Harrison pleaded.

Sapphire reached up and gently stroked his face.

"You can clean this mess," she answered. And with that, gathered her purse and strolled out. She closed her eyes and prayed he wouldn't follow her—and he didn't. Sapphire couldn't get away fast enough. Not because she felt hurt or ashamed, but because she had crossed a line, one that was supposed to separate business from pleasure. How on earth was she going to explain *this* to his wife?

Rule #1: Never sleep with a target.

Chapter 2

Be Careful what You Wish For

Where police officers worried themselves about criminals and bullets, firemen of fires, doctors of curing the sick, Sapphire faced an occupational hazard of her own… *dangerously handsome men*. It wouldn't be the first time, or the last. Occasionally she considered such dalliances a perk. But he was married. *MARRIED* for heaven's sakes, and that wasn't even the worst of it.

Sapphire dipped her toe into the bathtub before climbing in. After a rough night out, it was good to be home. She sunk down into scorching hot water and pushed the gargoyle shaped nozzle into the "on" position with her foot. The building, the city, were full of them. Gargoyles perched on top of skyscrapers were a common sight in her neighborhood. No one ever noticed them but she did…all of them; grotesque, frightening, and beautiful at the same time, her protectors watching over her. Where in the hell were they tonight? She hadn't quite, ever had an orgasm like that, not since Victor…

A burst of freezing water shot out of the faucet. Sapphire sunk into the depths of the water again, completely submerging as it continued to rise, then came bursting through the surface, gasping for air a few seconds later. Damn him! Damn him to hell! *Cheating bastard.* Of course, she'd known he was a cheater all along, after all, his wife was the one who hired her.

There was a reason why she didn't take such piddly jobs, and men like Harrison Brooks was it. She was supposed to catch Harrison in the act, photograph him leaving a hotel with some woman, and send the pictures to his wife. But he saw her first, and in true fashion, followed *her* to one of the lower floors in the library all the way down to the French literary section of all places. Who would find her there? She could shake him, right? She visited often, and certainly didn't expect him to enter her 'private' place. Harrison was every bit as mesmerizing as his wife described him, wolf in sheep's clothing that he was. He'd said it himself, he meets beautiful women in his spare time, and he'd met her that night, had her, and that was the end of it.

Sapphire wiped her eyes with the back of her hand and flipped the nozzle to the faucet down with her toe, shutting the water off. The water wasn't as hot anymore, and its healing powers seemed to have worked to great effect. She felt like a mermaid, foolish as that sounded… or better, she felt, *rejuvenated*. Maybe it was her mother and her grandmother's Creole blood running through her veins that made her believe in mythical and spiritual things such as gargoyles, mermaids, spells and healing waters.

Sapphire popped a birth control pill into her mouth, and went to bed that night, free of regret. She would find a way to tell Jane what happened. Well, the woman wanted proof that her husband was cheating, didn't she?

Be careful of what you wish for.

Sapphire's phone call the next day went as expected. She wanted to break the news to his wife, gently. If Jane was in love with Harrison, she would spare her the truth. If not, she would tell her what happened between them. She called later that afternoon. No need in ruining the woman's *entire* day.

"Hi Jane, how's everything going?"

She sounded awkward, even to herself.

"You have my pictures?" the woman interrupted.

"Not yet. I met him though."

"You were supposed to catch him in the act, not have a fucking discussion with him."

The few conversations she had with Jane revealed her to be a real *bitch*.

"I know."

"Then what in the hell did you talk to my husband about?"

"Harrison has a very *keen* eye. He saw me and talked to me first."

"Bitch, please…so you're on a first name basis with him now? You got sloppy. And I'm starting to feel like I'm dealing with an amateur."

Sapphire and Jane had yet to meet face to face. Had Jane seen her, Sapphire was sure she would not have hired her for the job. Sapphire kept her identity a secret from all of her clients, which had less to do with her looks, but her safety.

"I'm filing for divorce and I need to prove Harrison is having an affair or I get nothing because of an ironclad prenup. He cheated on me the entire marriage. He does not get to walk away scott-free. It's unfair! Your services came highly recommended. You're supposed to be an expert and yet you managed to blow your cover on the first day. What kind of shit is that?"

"It was an accident—" Sapphire started, knowing full well the excuse she'd given the woman was as pathetic as she sounded.

"Call me when you have the pictures," Jane impatiently replied.

"I'm not in the business of destroying families. I didn't sign up for that."

A bitter laugh filtered through the line.

"My marriage is none of your damned business, bitch. You act like you're screwing him. *Or did you?*"

Rule #2: Never get involved in the personal lives of your clients.

"It just happened..." Sapphire pleaded. "You said—he was attractive, and mesmerizing."

That sounded terrible, even to *her*.

"I don't give a fuck what I said. I wasn't paying you to fuck my husband. I hope lying on your back was worth it, bitch, because you're not getting a fucking dime until you prove my husband is the lying, cheating, scumbag I say he is. I want to bury that fucker and I mean, *BURY HIM*. Or do you think you're in love with him now, just like all of his other bitches?"

"I'm sorry about this, Jane. I don't know what to say. Maybe we should consider severing our business relationship…"

"No way—you fucking whore! You're going to see this all the way through to the end. I want the pictures. I don't care if it's you and Harrison, or some school girl. I gave him the best years of my life. I will *not*—I repeat, *will not*, walk away from this marriage empty-handed."

"I'll tail him today, get the pictures, and that'll be the end of it. You have my word. Just make sure you cut my check."

"Harrison's away on business."

"I travel."

"Not today you don't. He's in meetings all day in New Jersey. He won't have time to *rendezvous* with some pretty young thing. That's where the two of you are different. Harrison doesn't mix business with pleasure."

The situation with Harrison and his wife threatened the possibility of Sapphire ever returning to her former glory. She was a professional…***once***. It was bad enough her contemporaries no longer considered her at the top of her game. If word got back to them about this, she would officially become an industry joke…not that she wasn't already. A rendezvous wasn't necessarily a bad thing, in fact, it happened often in their line of work. A dalliance wasn't forbidden unless it happened to be with the spouse of a client or in the event that one of them was emotionally compromised. Blowing her cover on the first day was bad enough, but this… *this* was icing on the cake.

Sapphire wasn't into marital disputes, but it was her first job—in a while. Private detective work wasn't exactly what she wanted to do for a living but she was broke and there were debts in need of being repaid. Enemies who needed to suffer. Harrison was supposed to be a small job with big pay and Sapphire meant to see it through to the end, even if she liked him. Even if she couldn't stand his bitch of a wife.

Fresh-faced and dressed in jeans and a dark hoodie, Sapphire left her apartment a short time later, slipping into her black Audi R8 Spyder, which she kept parked at the back of a butcher's shop a block away. Rain poured down in sheets as she made her way down the road. She listened to the sound of the windshield wipers squeaking back and forth across the glass, and the pounding rain as she drove forty-five minutes away to a nondescript surveillance shop in the basement of a run-down electronics store in Queens. There were similar surveillance shops hidden in her neighborhood, but discretion was critical. She couldn't even park in front of her own apartment building... lest she wanted *the people she was hiding from,* to find her. Sapphire rented her apartment under an alias, and her Audi had been stripped of its VIN and replaced with one she'd purchased off the black market before registering it under the same name. Sapphire wasn't just a spy—but a corporate spy, driven out of the industry by *Elito,* her former employer, after falling madly in love with a target. It was a mistake she would never make again. Victor Reid had made it clear. He wasn't in love with her anymore, even though she sacrificed the assignment to protect him and his company.

"Thought they put you out of business," a gruff sounding voice called from behind the counter as Sapphire entered the shop. Rufio, peeked over a glass display filled with various electronics, much of it a mass of tangled wires, copper, ham radios, microchips, and car accessories. He sat on a bucket, shotgun across his lap as she locked the door behind her. The store smelled of cigars and a hint of car oil.

"You thought wrong, old man. I need surveillance equipment. Bugs, listening and tracking devices, the works."

"Much as I'd love to," he said, thick Italian accent almost unintelligible, "Domenico forbids it. He's still very angry with you, over that uh, job…" he said, waving a dismissive hand towards the door.

"He's still mad about that? It's not my fault they double booked us."

"Not *that* job. The diamond. He lost a lot of money. Won't do business with you. *And*," Rufio said, raising a finger in the air, "you owe us money."

Sapphire strode to counter with her arms raised as she approached the apprehensive old man.

"I'm good for it this time, Rufio…I swear."

"I can't give you another IOU."

"I don't need another IOU."

"Then how exactly do you intend to pay?"

Sapphire laid a black Amex card with the name "Samantha Reid", emblazoned across it onto the glass countertop.

Rufio stared at it a moment.

"What is this?" he asked, eyes squinting…as he took the information in.

"A credit card," Sapphire blinked.

Rufio laughed until he coughed up a throat full of mucus. He then spat into a handkerchief and wiped his mouth until the corners were dry.

"Pretty ballsy," he smiled. "I like you. I really do. But, *Domenico*…"

"—Please?"

Rufio gazed into her eyes for a moment, then rubbed a hand through what was left of his hair.

"Women…" he grumbled, waving irritably as he sat his shotgun on the floor.

Sapphire's heart pounded as she awaited Rufio's answer. He was an extremely difficult man to read, glaring at her with his beady bespectacled green eyes. As far as she was concerned, he could go either way. But he hadn't picked up the phone to receive the very handsome reward for her bounty…at least not yet, leaving Sapphire with little choice but to trust him.

The old man placed his hands atop the display and sighed heavily. "I've been warned not to do business with you. But it's not my place to get involved in other people's affairs. If you want to access my vault, you must first, say the magic words…"

"Really?"

"Yes, *really*," Rufio answered, eyes alight with mischief.

"That's so played out. I can't believe you guys are still doing that."

"We can't have just any old body coming in here, demanding technology that's not even on the market yet. Not even you."

Was he pulling her leg? Playing some sort of game with her? Did he really have what she needed or just the mass of copper wires and broken equipment on display? It could be a trap for all she knew.

"Then I suppose the password is still the same," Sapphire muttered, trying to get a read on the old man. The last thing she wanted was to disappear behind some locked door, never to be seen again. Can't trust anyone in this business...especially with so many people out there looking her. But it was a chance worth taking. She was almost out of money, and it was time to move on. Using Victor's credit card to pay for the equipment was a gamble she hoped would pay off.

"It's late March, year of the Fox," Sapphire said, taking a deep breath... "So the password must be, *Ex Astris Scientia*."

It was more of a question than an answer. She'd been a year and a half too long away from this sort of work. She'd told herself over and over again when she accepted Jane's assignment that it was dangerous—to get involved in any sort of spying again, even if it was just some private detective work. But she was in desperate need of the cash. She had to deliver this time. Sapphire wished she could disappear into an ordinary life like other people. Maybe work at a mom and pop store, bagging groceries, or at the library-even. But she wasn't good at anything else. What kind of skills did she really have, outside of dancing, and those days were long behind her. Deception was in her blood...a supernaturally acquired gift. Sapphire's eyebrows furrowed together as she awaited Rufio's response. He looked up, catching her eye, then pressed a button under the counter. A glass display case to her right slid to the side, revealing a darkened staircase.

"Come with me, *Gattina*."

Sapphire took a deep breath and followed the old man down the stairs to a dimly lit sub-basement. In her line of work, there were certain qualities you just don't lose, no matter how long you've been away. For Sapphire, it was confidence that kept her legs steady as they walked downstairs, despite the uncertainty before her. When they reached the bottom Rufio pressed a button, closing the entry upstairs. A pair of heavy metal doors slid open before them, revealing a high tech lab full of state of the art surveillance and spy equipment, a network of computers and white lab coat attired technicians. Various devices lay scattered about on tables, some of which were in pieces, others assembled, all of them objects she had never seen before. One of the technicians poked a mechanical crab-like robot with a pen, which caused it to spark, and one of its claws to snap at the young man's face.

"As you can see, we've made upgrades to some equipment you may have used at one time or another."

Rufio opened a display case filled with contact lenses.

"Do I need a prescription to wear one of these?"

"Maybe next time, Gattina. Which do you prefer, blue, green, brown?"

"Brown?"

He grabbed a set of contact lenses from the bottom shelf. "Brown it is."

Then opened the case.

"The latest in nano-technology," he said, holding the lenses before a florescent ceiling light. "This little device is worn in the eyes. It's what we call an opti-scan. Blink three times and it will scan an image of whatever you're looking at and download it to this wireless thumb drive. You'll need some time to adjust when you take them off. Surely you can use this in your line of work?"

Rufio gave her the thumb drive first, then the contact lenses.

"It's brilliant," Sapphire observed, examining the brown nano-sized computer chips coloring the contact lenses. "And exactly what I need. What about the listening device?"

"Of course. Follow me."

Rufio then turned to look at her in a very dramatic fashion.

"You'll find, young lady…that everything I have, is something else."

Before them, wall to wall surveillance monitors evaporated, like a holographic image.

"The secret to perfectly implemented espionage is the illusion of something being different from what it truly is."

Even the lab attendant standing before the holographic wall was a simulation, flickering as they walked through.

Sapphire trailed behind Rufio as he led her to the other side of a large storage room filled with electronic equipment and other ordinary supplies, and opened a metal filing cabinet. He reached into a drawer, retrieving a small black case filled with nuts and bolts.

"What am I supposed to do with this? Build a shelf?" She put her hands on her hips.

Rufio smiled. "See that nut?"

He pointed into the little black case.

"It's actually a bug… it looks like it belongs at the end of a shelf or a table, doesn't it? Stick it wherever you want. You'll find a headset and sound meter in the side panel."

"Thank you, Rufio. I really appreciate this."

"Stay out of trouble, that's all I ask."

"By out of trouble, you mean for me to stay out of business, I assume."

"You are dealing with some very dangerous people, *Gattina*. You're a sweet girl. I'd hate to see something happen to you."

"I'll be careful."

Sapphire collected the surveillance devices she needed from Rufio and paid with her black Amex card… thankfully before Domenico returned.

As she drove back to New York, Sapphire devised a plan to not only monitor Harrison, but also Jane. Whatever she could find about them both, she would use against them. The footage proving Harrison was a cheat, and included dirt on Jane that could be used to induce her to pay, if necessary.

Sapphire arrived at the Brooks' family home by nightfall, carrying only a reporter bag filled with surveillance equipment from Rufio's shop and her trusty survival kit filled with tools, knives, a flashlight, and medical equipment. Harrison and Jane lived in a tall, stately, three story house, with a big beautiful yard, sculpted hedges and a circular driveway.

She tiptoed around the bushes to the side of the house, sidestepping a water sprinkler, to a window where she heard male and female voices engaged in a heated discussion. Sapphire quickly retrieved a small dental mirror from her bag and pointed it at the window to see who was inside the house. The woman inside of the room was obviously Jane, caught in an embrace with a man that was not her husband. Sapphire smiled as she stuck a bug on the inside of the open window and used the sound meter to measure whether the recording was loud enough through her headset.

"What if your husband comes home?" the man said.

"He won't," Jane cooed. "After tonight, we won't have to worry about seeing him ever again. Nothing or no one will come between us."

"Damn it, Jane. What did you do?" the man snapped, pacing across the room.

"I hired someone.

"Someone to do what?"

"Someone to take him out," she answered coldly. "No courts, no prenup, just you, me and Harrison's money for the rest of our lives."

"Holy hell…" the man groaned. "I'm not getting involved with that. You have to stop it, Jane."

"He's sleeping with that private eye. She told him everything. I'll eventually have to deal with her too. She's the only one who knows."

"What about my son?"

"We can finally be together as a family, *John*…"

"I'm married, or did you forget that?"

Jane ran a finger down the front of John's shirt.

"About your wife…"

"What about her?"

"I told the hit man to use her as bait. After they lure Harrison next door to your house, I want him to shoot them both. Make it look like a robbery or a home invasion. It obviously can't look like a hit."

Sapphire pulled the headset off then leaned against the wall for support. People get divorced every day. Why would Jane want to kill her husband? Was it the money? Hate? Or pure evil?

She gathered her bag from the ground and put the contents back inside. Jane said Harrison was away in New Jersey for a business meeting. There was a reason why she wanted Sapphire to stay away and this was it. Jane had other plans, and worse, no intention of paying her anyway.

Gathering her equipment, ticked that she'd blown her wad at the surveillance store with Victor's credit card—and the fact that he might come after her as a result, Sapphire started towards the back of the house. Now that the money was off the table, Harrison and Jane was no longer her concern. To hell with them both—she could go home and look for other work. But as the depth of the situation hit her, Sapphire realized she no longer *cared* about the job or the money. Cheater or not, Harrison didn't deserve to die.

Besides…how much would Harrison pay for information about his wife?

A rustling of grass made Sapphire look up. She wrapped her bag over her shoulder and dropped to her knee, chest rising and falling sharply, as a shadow appeared before her in the distance. She'd been spotted—she was certain now, as the ominous figure looming in the shadows suddenly came into focus, a huge cloud of cigarette smoke floating around his gigantic head…a head, so large that it probably had its own gravitational pull. Had she been out of the business that long? How in the hell did she miss this guy, as big as he was?

"Don't tell me she double-booked us. You here to off the neighbor's wife or the husband?"

The hit man was right beside her now, gun lowered. Sapphire looked up, tried to make his features out in the darkness. He wore a suit and had long blonde hair that had been pulled into a ponytail. As her gaze rose to meet his, she tried not to show how nervous she was. Confidence had always been one of her greatest strengths. But this time her hands trembled, and her chest rose and fell sharply with each quickened breath. The last time she had a gun pointed at her face was a night she could no longer bear to remember. What to do? What to do? Her heart beat loudly in her ears….

The man regarded her for a moment, his eyes narrowing suspiciously as he took her in.

"Wait a minute..." the man said, lifting the barrel, which had a silencer attached. "Who the fuck *are* you?"

Sapphire's instincts kicked in faster than she could register her next heartbeat—she swiftly booted the weapon out of the man's hand, sending it flying, yards away into the bushes. He started after it and she took off, sprinting in the other direction. Sapphire crossed the neighbor's yard, leapt over a bush, and banked right—around the corner to her car. She heard the click of his gun in the distance and felt the wind behind the bullet as it sliced through the air over her shoulder. She opened the car door and climbed inside as a dark colored car screeched to a halt beside her. She looked out of her passenger side window. The hit man waved, and the car on the other side of her vehicle, which had nearly trapped her in, rolled the window down. She revved the engine up and took off as the passenger of the vehicle brandished a gun and fired. Thank heavens for bullet proof windows. The Toyota Camry the assassins drove was no match for her Audi Spyder. Something told her to use the hard top that day, otherwise, their bullets would have gone straight through her cloth convertible top.

Sapphire weaved in and out of traffic trying to shake the car in pursuit, but to no avail. Suddenly, three dark colored vehicles, one of them an SUV, coalesced behind her, the Toyota trailing behind them.

What the hell?

She tapped Brook Engineering into her GPS and hit the gas pedal. The Toyota soon fell away, but the three black vehicles remained in pursuit. She banked left then took an alleyway too narrow for the cars pursuing her to enter and when they went around to the other side, she shifted the Audi in reverse, and sped out, going back in the direction they came from. At last, she could breathe a sigh of relief. The three black cars were no longer behind her.

Sapphire followed the directions the GPS had given her to Brook Engineering, a large aviation engineering facility on the outer edge of the city. She drove down a secluded stretch of road to a parking lot outside of the main building but parked her vehicle behind a set of dumpsters just in case the hit men were still following her. She draped the reporter bag across her shoulder, put the optical-scan contact lenses in her eyes, and slipped into a pair of black leather gloves.

The building was dark. Was he still inside? She didn't know. Harrison struck her as the type of man who worked late—often, hence the problems with his wife and her ability to partake in an illicit affair right under his oblivious nose.

After a paranoid sweep of the area, Sapphire scampered out of the Spyder and sprinted across the parking lot until she reached a large glass door. With her back against the wall, she peered around the corner, and looked inside. There was a security desk in the dimly lit lobby, but where on earth was the guard? An alarm system outside of the building had been disarmed. Sapphire tried the door and to her surprise and bewilderment, found it unlocked. She tiptoed inside, pointing a flashlight into the darkness. A chill crawled up her spine. It was quiet. A little too quiet and still no security guard…which was unusual for a large facility at this time of night. Had they already gotten to them? Was Harrison even *alive*?

She had to find a way to reach him—a phone number, or some other means of contact to stop him from going home. And if all else failed, she'd call the police with the disposable cell phone in her bag.

Using her flashlight to see in the darkened building, Sapphire checked the directory on the lobby wall...names of company employees in rows of large white letters that looked like tiles from a game of Scrabble. As luck would have it, Harrison's office was on the bottom floor. She followed a sign next to the receptionist desk, which pointed to a range of offices that would lead her down a long dark corridor. At the end of it she saw a dim light filtering out of one of the rooms, and heard classical music—*Isabeau*, playing loudly. With the bag firmly attached to her side, Sapphire crossed her legs sideways as she eased down the hall. She could feel the vibrations of her heart thumping against her ribcage, as she crept towards the door, stooped low and peeked into the office, aiming the flashlight into a dark corner.

"Harrison?"

Thump. Thump. Thump.

Sapphire scanned the area, switching walls as she entered. It was a masculine office, with stark white walls and minimalist black furniture—desk, chair, table, lamps, and expensive artwork on the walls. A single picture frame enclosing a family portrait of Harrison, Jane, and a child who wasn't really his, sat next to yellow pencil holder. There was an adjoining bathroom, complete with a shower, and a small workout room. A workstation pushed against the wall supported a prototype of some kind. Sapphire blinked three times and scanned a photo of the component into her wireless thumb-drive, followed by successive images of the blueprints left on the table as she leaned across and turned the radio off.

"Harrison? You in here?"

Thump. Thump. Thump.

After a brief pause, she followed the thumping noise to a closet and slowly pulled the door open.

Seated on the floor with his hands tied behind his back and a strip of electrical tape over his mouth, was a plump middle-aged man wearing a blue and gold security guard uniform.

"Mrrrrm! Mrrrrmph!" he mumbled, shaking his head like he was possessed.

Sapphire ripped the tape from his mouth, stripping a large patch of facial hair with it.

"FUCK!" the man growled, looking like he wanted to rip her head off.

"Are you okay?"

"No—I'm not fucking okay, untie me."

"Where's Harrison?" Sapphire asked, ignoring the man's request.

"I don't know. Some guys disabled the alarm, walked right in and tasered me. They were looking for Mr. Brooks…may I ask who you are?"

He eyed her suspiciously.

"His bodyguard."

"A little lady like *you*?"

"I'm not the one who's tied up, buddy."

"Touché," he answered, as Sapphire flicked through the rope binding his arms with a pocket knife.

"Call the police, tell them Harrison might not make it through the night if they don't haul ass over to his house."

"Got it," the man said. "I talked to him earlier. He's on his way to the office."

"Good. I'll wait for him."

"What if the guys who tied me up come back?"

"Why are you asking me? You're the security guard! Reset the alarm codes and guard the building until the police arrive."

"Uh-right, got it."

The guard took off—his chunky body shaking like a bowl of Jello as he ran out the door.

Sapphire paced the floor, heart racing whenever she heard a sound. The clock ticking…pipes echoing... the security guard's footsteps moving down the hall. What will

Harrison say? What will he think when he see her face?

A light from the parking lot flashed into the window. Sapphire looked out. A silver BMW parked into a space near the entrance. She recognized the license plate number immediately—Jane had given it to her. Harrison stepped out of the car, and her heart skipped a beat. He looked taller, dressed in his blue business suit, intense brown eyes glaring ahead at the disabled alarm panel. He clutched his black briefcase like it was a prized possession and took quick long strides to the door. Seconds later, she heard a clamoring of footsteps and voices coming down the hall that grew louder as they neared the office. Remembering the contact lenses, Sapphire quickly took them out and put them back in the case. She blinked, her eyes blurring from the agitation. Rufio neglected to tell her the aftereffects of the lenses. Sapphire closed her eyes hoping the flashes of light and ghost codes would disappear. She gripped the side of the desk, as pain ripped through her head and the room started to spin. Suddenly, a pair of warm hands seized her by the arms, holding her steady.

"Did I fall asleep behind the wheel? Because I think I just died and went to heaven."

His gaze was warm. He looked so happy to see her. She fell into Harrison's open arms, her head resting against his chest.

Harrison had spent the past forty-eight hours looking for Sapphire and here she was, in his office as if fate had delivered her to him. He thought he'd never see her again. The woman was a ghost! With a name like Sapphire, he thought she would be easier to find. He'd forgotten that he told her where he worked, and that she could just as easily find him. Although, he wasn't exactly sure she'd want to after learning about his marriage to Jane.

He waited until she got her bearings, blinking until her pupils were no longer dilated.

"Are you okay?" he asked.

"I'm fine, just a little dizzy."

He released her and she drifted away, her posture upright again as she regained her strength.

"I missed you," he said.

She turned and looked at him, lips parting slowly, everything thing about her irresistible to him. Two quick strides across the room brought Harrison to her again. He swept Sapphire into his arms and lifted her up, his hands sliding wolfishly over her backside as he pushed her against the edge of his desk.

"Harrison, wait—" she started.

Sapphire pushed at his immovable frame…

"What are you doing here? I thought I would never see you again."

And he wouldn't have, if not for the circumstances, she thought. Oddly though, she was just as happy to see him.

"I didn't come here to talk about us."

Harrison gave her a quizzical look as he let her go.

"What else is there to talk about?"

"Your wife, she…"

"My wife and I are getting a divorce. I wanted to tell you that, but you left so quickly. You didn't give me a chance to explain."

"Harrison, I know, and that's what I want to discuss. I have something to tell you."

"I'm afraid you'll run out on me again, so please just let me say what I have to say and I promise to let you speak."

Harrison gripped her upper arms as if to keep her from leaving him again.

"When I was with you I felt more alive than I've felt in years. I know you think I'm a flirt and a cheating scumbag, but I never cheated on my wife. I need you to know that."

Sapphire shook her head. "What I think about your marriage doesn't matter."

"Of course it matters, you just won't admit it. I love that you play hard to get."

He cupped her chin and stroked her cheeks with the pads of his fingers.

"That's not what I mean," Sapphire started, slapping his hand away.

"I'm serious. I apologize if I did *anything* to hurt you or if you feel I took advantage of you in any way."

Harrison just didn't get it. He was trying to have a moment and she was trying to save his life! He was so hung up on connecting with her—or rather, sleeping with her again, that he was blind to the mounting danger surrounding them.

"I'm not hurt, Harrison. What I need is for you to leave the building with me, *now*."

She wanted to tell him about the hit but feared his reaction. Would he trust her, knowing Jane hired her to spy on him?

"As much as I want to I can't. I have work to do. *But*…we could always have fun here…"

Harrison pulled her towards him, his arms encircling her waist as their bodies collided. Sapphire couldn't tell if he was serious or not as she pressed her palms against his chest and pushed him away. Confused, he searched her eyes for answers, before finally letting her go.

"I found your security guard in the closet with his hands tied behind his back."

"And you just happened to be here to rescue him?"

He lifted a brow.

"Andre told me about the break-in, we've had them before. Reinforcements are on the way to help him lock the rest of the facility down. Don't worry, we'll get it sorted."

Sapphire grabbed the phone from his desk and handed it to him. "Let the police sort it and get out of here. I'll dial them for you myself if I have to."

Harrison loosened his tie. "We prefer to handle these matters, internally, if you don't mind."

"You're not listening to me, are you? If you don't' get out this building, you're a dead man…."

Sapphire grabbed Harrison's arm and pulled him towards the door, but he jerked her back, yanking her arm with him. He gazed fiercely into her eyes, his cool brown gaze turning cold.

"Is that why you're dressed in black? Because someone sent you here to kill me?"

"If I wanted to kill you, you would already be dead."

He should have known it was too good to be true, to meet a beautiful woman, who actually wanted or cared about him. Hurt and anger shaded his eyes as he glared down at her lovely face, wondering what he'd done to deserve her treachery. Sapphire started towards the door.

"You can stay here if you want, I did what I could to help you…and that includes risking my own life."

No sooner than her words were spoken, a loud crack shattered the silence, followed by a succession of bullets piercing Harrison's window. Sapphire instinctively ducked, as a bullet sliced through the air and knocked him on his back. Harrison whipped his head to the side, blood seeping from an open wound near his temple.

Sapphire scrambled across the floor on her knees as the room went black, the power shutting down around them.

"Harrison?" she panted frantically, grasping blindly for him in the darkness.

"What the hell…" he groaned. "Fucking bullet grazed my head. Got'damned thing damn near took my eye out."

"We have to get out of here. Follow me."

The two of them crawled out of the office on their knees to the hallway. There, Harrison used the wall for support as he stumbled to his feet, leaving a bloody handprint on the stark white wall.

"Hurry!" Sapphire wailed, unable to hide the quiver in her voice. She was used to looking after herself, but looking after someone else was a different matter.

Confidence firmly shattered, Sapphire started down the hall towards the lobby for a quick escape when Andre, the security guard appeared out of the shadows clutching his gun, his body pressed against the wall. He waved her back. She dove to the side and felt a sharp pain ripple through her leg. Her knee buckled, her old dance injury resurfacing at exactly the wrong time. Sapphire cried out, wincing as she leaned against a beam for support.

Harrison hissed, calling her back as a clattering of footsteps moved towards his office.

"There's an emergency exit around the corner."

He pulled Sapphire in the opposite direction. They made a hasty escape down a maze of hallways and exited through the loading dock. Harrison knew the building like the back of hand. Unless the attackers had a floor plan, which he doubted, it would be hard to track them, especially now that they were on the outside running away from the building.

"My car is just behind the dumpsters."

Harrison came to an abrupt stop, his eyes glaring after her as she limped ahead of him towards the Spyder.

"And why should I trust you?" he sneered.

"Ten minutes ago you couldn't live without me," Sapphire retorted

"That was before you told me about the hit. And you still have yet to explain your role in all of this and how you came to know about it."

"I'll explain everything in the car."

"I'll take my own, thank you!"

"Supposing, it doesn't blow up when you start the engine or some sniper's bullet doesn't hit its target this time."

Harrison sighed and wiped the blood from his eye with the sleeve of his jacket.

"You're out of your league," Sapphire stated, turning away.

"*And you aren't?*" Harrison retorted.

Sapphire used a keyless entry device to start the car remotely. The engine purred to life, the xenon headlights flickering on, bathing them in blue light.

They raced to the vehicle.

Sapphire unlocked the doors and the two of them climbed into the car. She could feel Harrison's icy gaze on the side of her face as she buckled herself in. Instead of poking his eyes out, she focused on a commotion of vehicles entering the parking lot as she peeled rubber and veered around the dumpster to the nearest exit. She swerved around a pair of cars, and a gang of armed hit men blocking the only exit as Harrison fumbled with his seatbelt.

"You might want to duck, now!"

Harrison lowered himself into the passenger seat and covered his already bloodied head as a hail of bullets rang out behind them.

"Seriously! Who in the hell *are* you?" he squealed, the car throwing him against the door as it did a 360 in the middle of the highway and sped away in the opposite direction.

Sapphire ignored him and focused on the road. They drove a great distance before she poked her head up and looked in the rearview mirror. One of the vehicles had started after them. She hit the gas pedal and the car surged, leaving the hit man's car in its dust... but not before two dark vehicles coalesced in front of the other vehicle, blocking its pursuit of her car.

Realizing the danger was far behind them now, Harrison finally sat up.

"You got some explaining to do."

Sapphire kept smoky eyes on the road.

"Your wife hired me to spy on you."

"Why?"

"She was looking for ammunition to use in the divorce."

"Did she hire you to fuck me too?"

Harrison's frosty gaze sent a chill running up her spine. Sapphire focused on the lines of the road with laser-like precision, avoiding his piercing glare.

"We had a very passionate night but it wasn't planned. You followed me, remember?"

"I saw you lurking around the bar. I thought you were after something."

"I was. Just not what you thought I was after," she answered.

Harrison grabbed the steering wheel and pulled it to the right, causing them to veer to the side of the now deserted road onto low ground.

"We can't stay here," she warned.

He turned the headlights off as pairs of cars zoomed by in succession seconds later. "Problem solved," he countered, eyeing a vehicle carrying a couple of hit men as it passed them by.

"So this is the part-time job you didn't want to tell me about?"

"Sort of…" she replied.

"What are you? A private eye? Some kind of a spy?"

Harrison clenched his teeth so forcefully she thought they would crack.

"Some kind of a spy," Sapphire finally admitted, after a deep breath.

"A spy or an *assassin*?"

He glared at her now.

"You're still here, aren't you? I had nothing to do with hiring hit men to kill you if that's what you're asking. That was all Jane," Sapphire said, throwing her hands in the air. "I was supposed to take pictures, and do a little private detective work for her…that's it."

"Take pictures of what?"

"She wanted to catch you in the act."

"I'm not the one who's cheating," Harrison sneered.

"Yeah, I'm kind of figuring that out now. It was just a job, Harrison, nothing personal."

"You mean it wasn't personal to *you*. It was very personal to me. Everything you ever told me was a lie. Why should I believe you now?"

Sapphire opened her bag and fished around for the recording of Jane and handed it to him.

She waited as Harrison listened to the device, realizing his entire life was soon to be turned upside down. From his wife's affair, the plot to kill him, and the possibility that the boy he thought he fathered, might not being his.

Sapphire reached across Harrison's seat and held his hand in hers as the minutes rolled by, his shoulders slowly sagging as the recording played. When it finally ended, Harrison gave the listening device back to Sapphire, his gaze askew, fingers absently tracing the outline of his lips.

"I'm sorry," she finally offered.

But Harrison turned away, his gaze focused on the red-orange foliage outside of the car. He would *show her sorry*, he thought, with a mental scoff.

"Take me home—somewhere," Harrison demanded, unsure where home even was, now.

Sapphire gave him her disposable cell phone.

"I think you know what you need to do…"

With a defeated look in his eyes, Harrison pressed the speaker button and reluctantly dialed '9-1-1'. A faint masculine voice crackled onto the line, immediately.

"Dispatch, 9-1-1," the operator said.

"My name is Harrison Brooks. I need an officer at 7568 Cherry Lane."

"What's the problem sir?"

"Someone is trying to shoot me."

"Are you injured?"

"Yes, a flesh wound on my head."

"Are the attackers nearby? Are you at the residence now?"

"No, sir. My wife hired a hit man to have me killed. I don't see myself returning any time soon."

"Harrison Brooks, you say?"

"Yes, that is correct."

"Are you able to hold for a moment, sir?"

"I am safe for the time being, but please do hurry."

Harrison glanced up to find Sapphire's twitchy fingers clutching the steering wheel, her foot ready to hit the gas at the first sign of danger. Tendrils of her hair had fallen loose from her ponytail into long wavy coils on the nape of her neck. Oh, how he had itched to brush them away...to graze her warm soft skin with his lips. She tilted forward and looked up at the road for the hit men again with large brown eyes that saw everything, but him. The ice on Harrison's heart melted. She could have walked away after the recording of Jane but instead chose to find him and warn him about his wife, even putting her own life at risk to save him. Was she mysterious? *Yes.* Deceitful? *Definitely.* Sneaky? *Even more so.* But her good qualities far outweighed the bad...Sapphire only needed to channel her negative traits into positive ones. The past few days had been more exciting than anything that had ever happened to him in his entire life. Was it foolish that he envisioned a future with Sapphire? That he could see himself falling in love with her someday?

"Mr. Brooks?" The dispatcher called, disrupting his thoughts. "Detective Colton will meet you at your residence. How soon can you be there?"

"Did you hear what I said? There's a hit man at my house waiting to kill me."

"We're aware of the situation, Mr. Brooks. We'd like to talk to you."

His gaze shifted to Sapphire.

"I don't trust anyone right now."

"Would you prefer to meet us at the 5th Precinct?"

"I can meet Detective Colton there in twenty minutes."

"Thank you, sir. Please call back if you need us and be sure to keep your cell phone turned on should we need to locate you."

"Can we go now?" Sapphire queried, as soon as the dispatcher hung up.

Harrison held her intense gaze with one of his own.

"Yes, thank you for taking me."

Sapphire took Harrison to a police station some short ten or fifteen minutes away and parked in front of a building teeming with criminals and police officers alike. They were all crooks, as far as she was concerned. Sapphire resented the police officers who, over the years pursued her like bloodhounds, while protecting some slimy corporation's investment, instead of using the city's resources to protect the innocent from crime.

Eighteen months ago Sapphire made her fortune stealing trade secrets from corporations. She used to think she was doing the world a service, so that one behemoth billion dollar company couldn't monopolize a useful invention, whether the product was a technical invention, a pharmaceutical product that saved lives or seeding agriculture used to monopolize the farming industry. Her first assignment as a corporate spy was through a shadow agency called Elito. She had been called to infiltrate an agricultural giant that specialized in selling seeds to farmers, but refused to allow use of seeds resulting from a season's yield, through the use of intimidation, coercion and the legal system. Sapphire managed to infiltrate the company as a cleaning lady, gaining access to restricted areas and classified documents. She then copied the stolen data and sold it to a competitor that highly favored the farmers, allowing them use of seeds from their crops. In the end, it was a win for the poor farmers of the world and an even bigger win for common decency. Sapphire had used evil to achieve good, and the results were highly gratifying. She was Robin Hood, stealing from the rich to give to the poor.

As the head of an engineering corporation, Harrison was no different from the men she regularly stole from. But tonight, he was a human being.

"Need me to walk you to inside?" Sapphire asked, pulling the hoodie she wore back onto her head.

Police stations made her jumpy with their spy cams and face identification software, but she was willing to see him to safety.

"Gorgeous *and* brave…" Harrison grinned, his unwavering gaze trained on her face. "But I'll be fine."

"So I guess this is goodbye," Sapphire smiled.

"Only if you want it to be," he countered, turning in his seat to face her.

"I wish you the very best…take care, Harrison."

"You don't have to settle for this life. I can give you everything you ever wanted," Harrison whispered.

Sapphire started the engine.

"That's what they all say," she replied.

"We've had a strange journey…among other things. That should count for something, right?"

Harrison's eyes lit up as Sapphire gently caressed his cheek with one of her hands, her finger tips brushing the back of his dark wavy hair. She resisted kissing him as she gazed into soft brown eyes overflowing with desire and need. He kissed the palm of her hand, inhaling the fresh beauteous scent of her skin as she pressed her forehead against his.

"You are a beautiful man," Sapphire said, her fingers stroking the back of his hair and neck. "But you need time."

"I don't want time, I want *you*," he answered.

Harrison pulled her to him and kissed her deeply, his heavy chest leaning from his seat into hers. She could feel his passion spilling into her in every breath as he drew her into his muscular arms, his mouth, full and warm covering hers. But Sapphire pushed away, unable to stand the violent wash of need that flushed into his eyes. A look that subjected her to feelings she couldn't identify. She'd tried love, she'd tried being in a relationship, and in the end had been burned.

Harrison buried his face into the side of her neck and traced his lips down to the swell of her breasts. Sapphire held him close, melting into the gentle caress of his lips against her skin. His warm flesh against hers, head cradled in her arms, the night's trauma slowly faded away.

He lay there a moment, ear against her beating heart, his breaths heavy. When he finally looked up, Sapphire pointed at the glass police station door.

Inside, a very sleepy three year old little boy clung to the hand of a uniformed officer and a stuffed animal.

Harrison wondered why his son was at the police station, and not with his mother or the nanny? He moved away from Sapphire, unlocking the car door.

"I will be waiting at the library where we first met, on the stairs next to the entrance, tomorrow at six o'clock. If you show up, we'll pick up where we left off. If not, I'll respect your wishes and leave you alone, forever…."

Then with a fleeting look said, "I hope to see you there."

He kissed her again then exited the car. Sapphire watched as Harrison raced into the building, hoisted the boy into his arms, and kissed him on the forehead.

Jane was arrested not long after confessing her scheme to John, though not in time to cancel the hit on Harrison's life, until being forced to do so by the detective handling the investigation. Turns out, John wasn't keen on Jane's plan to kill his wife and turned her in.

Harrison went home with his son that night, no longer afraid of who might be lurking in the shadows, not caring if the boy was his biological son. He'd raised him from birth. Unlike Jane, he knew how to love, and that was all that mattered.

With Harrison safe and in the hands of the NYPD, Sapphire drove straight home. She felt leery however, speeding through the now deserted dimly lit streets. There were only a few cars on the road, three of which, she had seen earlier in the day, when a trio of black cars pursued her—twice, cutting the other vehicles off in a high speed chase with the hit men. She had a feeling, these guys weren't after Harrison... they were after her.

Sapphire parked in her usual spot—in a shadowy cove behind the butcher shop, but took an alternate route to her cramped sixth floor apartment a block away. She climbed a fire escape to the roof, her busted knee throbbing with pain as she hoisted herself onward and upward to heights that would make a grown man wet his pants.

Under a cloak of darkness, she crossed the closely situated rooftops not unlike a shadow, scrambling deftly along the loosened pebbles strewn across the flat rooftop, until she made it safely to her building. With the wind sweeping her hair into a state, she crouched at the edge of the roof and looked down at the traffic below, her foot propped high on the brick surround. The trio of black vehicles circled the block on separate street corners before coalescing into a row along the curb a half block away, lights dimmed. She smiled, knowing they would never find her. Sapphire's apartment, with its brick wall for a window, was impenetrable.

She opened a hatch in the roof, hung, and dropped the short distance to the floor, grunting as pain ripped through her knee.

The first thing Sapphire did upon entering her apartment was strip out of her clothes and run a bath. She was in dire need of its healing powers tonight. She knew, once the knee went out, it would be days, sometimes weeks before it healed again. So she climbed into the tub and immersed her aching body into the scalding hot water. Her apartment seemed especially quiet…filled with the kind of deafening silence that made her ears hurt. Five years ago, an intense yearning for adventure led her down this dark and lonely path, at a time when she was at her most broken, and vulnerable. A simple lift from her dance partner, and an intentionally misplaced foot had left her in the hospital for weeks with a shattered knee and metal pins in her leg. The recovery process for her physical ailments had taken months. But the emotional damage…well, she was still working on that. Sapphire's career as a ballet dancer had been promising. There was even talk she'd someday make prima ballerina. Dancing was her life. Sapphire lived it, breathed it, from the moment she awakened until she fell asleep at night, bruised and battered from hours of intense practice. She remembered soaring...the wind in her hair, before her wings had been clipped so cruelly, mid-flight.

News of her accident traveled lightning-fast through the dance community...bundled with rumors detailing the extent of her egregious injuries. So it didn't take long for peers and dance choreographers alike, to blithely write her off before the rehabilitation process could even begin. The ballet profession very rigidly demanded perfection of its adherents. And when Sapphire *could* walk again, she did so, with a limp.

In a few weeks—the world would move on without her. The balloons, get-well cards, and the flowers dwindled, as did the phone calls and visits. And then there was no one...except the benefactor, who'd graciously covered her medical expenses, rehabilitation, and salvation...in exchange for a few years of service. After some initial hesitation, Sapphire realized she had nothing to lose in accepting their offer. Her only living relative was an ailing grandmother, who could barely remember her name. She had no money. And her friends—if you could call them that, were other dancers, and only cared about their own advancement.

So she made new friends. Tennessee Jenkins was her name…the tall, statuesque director of the secretive corporate spy network, *Elito*. She had blonde hair, chubby cheeks, and a stubborn southern accent as thick as her big legs. Her appearance was very ladylike, and her style made her the epitome of a southern belle. Tennessee was pleasant enough, with her megawatt smile and soothing manner, even when she peppered her words with the occasional threat. She was the kind of woman you expected to pass out hugs and sage advice, rather than assignments to spy on elite companies or threats to ruin you and your family. Sapphire was suspicious at first, wondering why Elito would want to recruit a badly crippled dancer into their agency…until she received her first assignment, and a picture of Belinda Simpson. The ballet rival who had caused her onstage fall was the niece of a high ranking executive at an agricultural corporation. Tennessee lured Sapphire in with the oh-so-sweet promise of revenge. So sweet, Sapphire could still taste it, four years later. Even though a successful mission could never pay Belinda back for what she did, a proper comeuppance was long overdue.

And yet, Belinda's betrayal had been a curse *and* a blessing…for exposing the long arduous hours at the studio and opera house, hard slept nights, and early morning practice sessions since the age of five, had allowed Sapphire to neglect; life, friendship, and love. Though love, wasn't something she knew much about, as she hadn't experienced it firsthand until she met Victor Reid. Without Belinda, they never would have met and Sapphire would never have known what it felt like to be in love, no matter how fleeting. Eighteen months later, she still longed for Victor with an intensity that made her chest ache, even though he wanted nothing to do with her now. The second he learned about her connection to Elito and that she had been contracted to steal from Reid Robotics, it was over.

Victor worked as hard as he loved and loved as strongly as he hated. And he hated *her*. Tennessee warned Sapphire about getting too close to a target, and when she finally realized she'd been emotionally compromised, it was too late. How could she betray the man she loved? How could she steal his life's work, his life's passion? Sapphire wanted out of Elito, and out of the job, but they refused to let her go. Tennessee didn't give a rat's ass about her engagement to Victor Reid, that they were living together, or that Sapphire was done with spying for good. It wasn't over until Elito wanted it to be over. Sapphire's mistake was believing her own lies, and that the fantasy of a 'happily ever after' with Victor was ever possible.

Then the blackmailing began. She was to give Elito the data they wanted from Reid Robotics or they would deliver a file to Victor's doorstep, telling him everything; that her life as executive secretary, Samantha Cole, had been a complete lie. Or as Tennessee phrased it…that she was just another "treacherous scamp looking for a bigger payday."

Little did they know, Sapphire didn't care about Victor's wealth…she cared about *him*. It wasn't the parties, the gifts, the house, or the glamorous life she'd they shared, but the endless nights in his arms. Feeling safe, complete, and loved for the first time in her miserable life…and Elito was willing to take that away. They made her, and they would damn sure, break her.

In her desperation, Sapphire stole an encrypted outline to Victor's billion dollar research project, having no idea what it entailed. A project so covert, employers needed high-level security clearance and were required to submit a DNA sample just to access his laboratory. To stay together, she'd done the one thing that would rip them apart.

Sapphire unplugged the bathtub and climbed out. Harrison's proposition had left her feeling vulnerable. And at her most vulnerable, she always thought of Victor. Could she have a life with Harrison? Could she leave her shady past behind, to take care of him and his little boy?

The idea was tantalizing, but Sapphire was in too much pain to think on it further. So she turned the faucet on, popped a couple of Vicodin she found in the medicine cabinet into her mouth, and drank water pouring into the palm of her hand from the bathroom sink until the pills went down. After wrapping her swollen knee in Kinesio tape she plopped into bed, still wrapped in her bath towel, and laid down. Her mind eventually falling into a drug induced haze, Sapphire very slowly fell asleep, wondering... could she? *Would she, meet Harrison tomorrow? Was it too late to start over?*

Chapter 3

Warm flesh

Streams of light beamed through the cracks of a brick wall outside of a window that was Sapphire's view. She loved the darkness, and the slivers of light peeking into her room as she snuggled under a blanket to keep warm, shielding herself from the cool air blowing inside. Her eyelids felt heavy from the Vicodin, which allowed her to sleep late, with hopes of rising when the sun disappeared behind a dark amber-orange horizon. She felt warmer than usual, her cheek pressed against warm flesh as she stirred, moving to turn in her sleep.

Warm flesh?

Sapphire's eyes fluttered open, resisting the pull of the painkiller's spell. Her face lay against the smooth curve of a man's stomach, drool spooling from the corner of her mouth into a tiny puddle onto his skin. Was she that high on Vicodin that she'd gone out and brought someone home? The man slept soundly, his chest rising and falling deeply, barely audible snore rumbling at the back of his throat.

An intruder? In her fortress? Sapphire eased to the side of the bed, reaching under the mattress for a knife she'd hidden there, but a firm hand gripped her upper arm, holding her in place as if he had already contemplated her next move.

Then she heard it, a familiar British accent.

"Still utterly, predictable. I've already removed them, all of your weapons."

He crushed her shoulders together, pulling her up. How the hell did he get in here?

Sapphire struggled-fought, to say something—to get the words out, but could do nothing but stammer, as she stared wide-eyed at his face, wondering if she were dreaming. Then he smiled, crippling her with that disarming, boyish grin.

"When you look at me that way I almost believe you love me," Victor said, his sulky mellow voice dropping to an even sexier timbre.

"What are you doing here?" Sapphire asked, unsure of how to respond.

Beneath Victor's cool, ice cold gaze lie whirling pools of disappointment. She *did* love him, he had to know that, or did he?

He gripped her face with his hand, the pad of his thumb burrowing into her cheek as he yanked her face upward.

"We had a deal."

"It's not a deal when the agreement is forged under duress."

"Meaning?"

"When you twist someone's arm, forcing them to agree…"

"It wasn't your arm that I wanted to twist," Victor sneered, fingers sliding down to her neck. "When I learned the woman I planned to marry conspired to prize my life's work away."

He pressed his thumb against the center of her throat. Sapphire swallowed as she brushed it aside.

"Everything you ever told me was a lie," he said, voice dangerously low.

"Not everything," Sapphire murmured.

When Victor's highly mercenary security team caught Sapphire stealing the encrypted research data from the laboratory, the first thing she felt was the brunt end of a soldier's rifle smashing into her gut. They roughed her up then dragged her to an abandoned warehouse, where she was not only slapped around, but had endured endless hours of psychological torture until she confessed, under extreme duress to being a spy. Why did she come back in the first place after she had already escaped? The warehouse was badly lit, grey, with vaulted glass ceilings filled with broken windows. The spacious interior was some thirty or forty degrees icier than it was outside. Sapphire trembled, hands tied behind her back where she was forced to stand until her legs were tired. The knee couldn't take it so she eventually broke down and kneeled, curling into a ball on the cold concrete floor, with only her breath to keep her warm.

The men used every tactic imaginable—from pretending that they would execute her, to subjecting her to humiliating forms of physical abuse, all with hopes of coercing her into compromising the contract, and her employers. But Sapphire refused, fearing Elito more than the armed men surrounding her. They wanted to know what she knew, who hired her, and who she'd talked to…Sapphire tried to explain how much she loved Victor, and didn't want to betray him, but no one listened.

What hurt her most was learning Victor had not only known about the torture, but sanctioned the interrogation in advance. Elito had given him her file before she attempted to steal the data, so he had already bitterly anticipated her impending betrayal, and never let her forget it.

Rule #3: Never fall in love with a target.

"You were compromised. Your file sent to the security detail of every corporation in my network and beyond. You were released from capture on the condition that you leave New York and espionage behind you. And yet, here you are, as if nothing ever happened."

He shook his dark head in disbelief.

"I'm not a spy. Not anymore. You saw to that," Sapphire answered, gathering the red colored bed sheet around her.

"Then take your fortune and leave," Victor hissed.

"I can live wherever I want. You don't own New York!" Sapphire fired back.

"Don't I?"

She met his fiery gaze.

"You have no *right*…to force me out. New York is *not* your territory and I did nothing wrong."

"Except that you're up to the same old tricks. I've been watching you."

"Then you might have noticed I was minding my own business until *you* broke into *my* apartment."

"Is that what you were doing at the surveillance shop? Minding your own business?"

"Not all of us are billionaires like you. I have to earn a living. It was for a job, Victor. Some private detective work."

"And what a splendid job you're doing. You almost got the poor guy killed."

"He's alive now, isn't he?"

"He wouldn't be, if I hadn't sent my security team to intervene."

"I don't need your help!" Sapphire snapped.

She gathered the sheet around her and rolled out of bed, exposing his bare torso and legs. A blanket lay stretched across his lap, concealing what was beneath. She prayed, for his sake, there were underpants on that body of his.

Victor grabbed her arm and pulled her back.

"I wasn't offering my help," he scoffed. "At least not to you... I won't let you do what you did to me to that man and his kid."

"Like you give a shit about *him*. Is that what this is about? The second another man enters my life, you magically appear? Are you jealous that I might have a stable relationship, life, and love with someone other than you? Well, you're worrying yourself over nothing. I barely know the man."

"It's about you being an evil, lying, manipulative little bitch. I won't let you destroy this man's life the way you destroyed mine."

"I didn't destroy you," Sapphire gasped. The back of her eyes felt hot. "I loved you…"

"You loved me? *You loved me so much*, that you lied to me for over a year about who you were? That you stole my life's work and very nearly sold it to my competitor, then disappeared without a trace? If that's love, then I'd hate to be your enemy. Oh! I forget. I already was."

"I left because you told me to!"

"You should have begged my forgiveness."

He still held tight to her arm.

"If you hate me so much then why are you here?" Sapphire sniffed, tears filling her eyes.

"I may hate *you*," he said, "and the lying bitch that you are…but I still love Samantha Cole."

Sapphire tried averting her eyes from Victor's dark hypnotic gaze, but found herself unable to look away as he leaned in and kissed her so intensely, she couldn't breathe. But then, kissing Victor Reid had always left her feeling breathless, even if they hated each other. Sapphire was still very much in love with the sweet, handsome, adoring man she'd met at

Reid Robotics three years ago. They even kissed the same. But they were not the same men. Victor was a shadow of the person he used to be. She no longer recognized him in the vindictive, angry monster he'd become. Had she made him that way? Or had he too, worn a mask from the very beginning?

This was a man with paid mercenaries to protect, with deadly force, whatever research he deemed too important to slip from his grasp. *That* man, had always existed, even before he learned she was a spy. Victor was as ruthless and heartless a business man as any, and had now unleashed his endless venom upon her. But the man Sapphire wanted, the man she loved was still in there, somehow…even if she couldn't see him. Just as she was in Samantha Cole. She *was* Samantha Cole…

Sapphire held Victor's face between the palms of her hands and searched his eyes for an inkling…of him, tiny flickers of the lovely man she once knew hidden beneath the vortex of dark emotions whirling there. He reached for the knot that held the sheet wrapped around her in place, pulled the material away, and stared in awe, of the soft glow of her skin, dark, golden, and majestic in the flickering streams of sunlight. Sapphire moved the blanket from his lap and heard him draw his breath from the electric feel of her touch as she stroked his hardened flesh. He scooted back, and she crawled forward, climbing onto his lap, clamping her legs around him. Victor controlled every aspect of his life, but in the bedroom, he relinquished control, kissing her exposed nipples until they were hard and moist from the warmth of his mouth. Sapphire raked her fingers down his chest, lower still until the armor guarding his heart fell, as she stroked, and massaged until he'd all but begged her to take him. They lay a coiled mess, their bodies like pieces of red-hot coals rubbing together at the bottom of a fiery pit.

Despite the enmity emanating between them, making love to Victor was a pleasure she could no longer deny herself as he placed his hands on her waist and she positioned herself above him, moaning as he slowly, tenderly, entered her, gazing into Victor's now crystal clear eyes. She immediately rocked back and forth, meeting his frenzied thrusts, lips licking and nipping, their slick, sweaty physiques writhing together in this manner until something within her broke. He whispered something, something about loving her still. He said he loved her and Sapphire wanted to believe him. It was in his eyes when he looked at her. In his touch, when he caressed her. *I love you too…*

She convulsed, ripples of pleasure pulsing violently throughout her body at the thought, with Victor sighing, and moaning as he soared to momentum shortly after. She then rolled to her hip, lying beside him, torn between the fiery passionate moment they'd jointly shared, and the reality of the tumultuous past that tore their hearts asunder. He couldn't even look at her now, and in fact, seemed ashamed of his indiscretion. Victor lay on his back, hands absently roaming up and down his chest as he gazed at the ceiling, thoughts awry.

"Have you ever really loved anyone?" he asked, narrowing his eyes to tiny impenetrable slits.

"You know I did."

"I'm not sure you're capable. Not that it's your fault, or the fault anyone who might have been reared by an unaffectionate old grandmother."

He smirked then, putting his hands behind his head as he reclined on one of her pillows.

"Have you ever been loved?"

"No, I don't think I ever was," she answered, firm in this belief now.

Victor sat up, eyes glaring.

Sapphire rolled out of bed, grabbing the closest article of clothing she could find, a nightshirt she'd laid out to wear the night before. She felt the heat of Victor's gaze trained on her back as she walked to the kitchenette.

"For once in your rotten life," he said, "will you show me who you really are?"

Sapphire paused… steps away from the kitchen, her back facing him.

"What do you want from me?" she asked, shoulders slumping.

"Show me who you are. You're a cripple aren't you? Then walk like one."

Tears stung the corners of her eyes. Victor's cruelty was unbearable. He would never forgive her, no matter what transpired. She knew that now. Sapphire continued on, adopting a natural limp as she abandoned the posture she'd carefully assumed to conceal her painful leg injury. Still feeling the heat of Victor's gaze on her back, she stopped at the kitchen sink, filling a glass of water.

"Is that what you wanted to see?" she asked him, bitterly.

"I only ever wanted to see the real you."

"You would never accept the real me, I know that now."

Her shoulders slumped further still, she had never felt so utterly defeated. So heartbroken... there was no future with Harrison, Victor would see to that. Not because he loved her, or wanted her, but to ruin her chance at happiness.

"You don't have to worry about Harrison, or his son. You win. I've decided to leave New York."

She spent the last eighteen months running from Elito and Victor. Had he known where she was the entire time? Sapphire heard the bed creak behind her as Victor rolled off, his feet landing with a thud on the hardwood floor.

"And go where?" he asked, his voice like silk, as he approached from behind, sliding his arms around her waist.

How could someone so cold feel so warm?

"Does it matter? I'm sure you'll have no problem finding me."

"I always do," he answered, kissing Sapphire tenderly behind the ear.

He walked away, snatching his clothes up from the floor in haste before swiftly slipping into his pants and button down shirt, looking ever the smart business man.

She turned to catch him counting a stack of bills in his wallet. He tossed them on the bed.

"This should help get you on your way," he muttered tersely, "Should you need it."

He watched her from the side of his eyes as the cash fell to the bed.

"I don't want your money," Sapphire snapped.

"—Is that so? Because I'm fairly certain, *Samantha **Reid**,* would beg to disagree. I know your next move before you think about it."

Sapphire's stomach clenched into a knot.

Victor tucked his hands into his pockets and looked at the floor, a vein streaking down the center of his forehead like a bolt of lightning.

"You look surprised," he observed, peeking at Sapphire's now frozen face. "How else do you think I would have found you? Or am I mistaken in thinking that's exactly what you wanted?"

"I want for us not to hate each other anymore," Sapphire answered.

"That's not going to happen," Victor smiled. "After being so superbly deceived by the likes of *you*…not for a time."

"You could always move on with your life."

"I'm having too much fun for that," Victor beamed.

"Fun at my expense."

"And you, mine."

He stood gazing at her as she leaned against the sink, watching as he prepared to leave.

"I have just one question before you go," Sapphire blurted.

A curious gleam materialized in Victor's eyes. "Why did you stay the night? Why would you *sleep* with me?"

She wouldn't finish the rest… which was to ask, why he would do those things if he hated her so much…

Victor shrugged, meandered thoughtfully towards the door with his jacket slung over his shoulder, hooded eyes cast towards the floor.

"That…was for me," he answered, coldly. "*Whore.*"

Her heart sank.

Victor just couldn't bring himself to leave without striking a final blow. Sapphire closed her eyes to shut out the pain that enveloped her as he walked out the door.

Depression hit Sapphire hard. She climbed into bed, curling into a ball, where she stayed for hours, unable to sleep or move. But as evening approached she knew, she'd have to find the strength to rise….

She showered, then packed her bags, leaving everything she couldn't pack into the Spyder behind, carrying with her, a couple of handbags, money, and a few pieces of clothing.

Of course, she'd eventually have to get rid of the Spyder too. Victor had probably used the vehicle to track her. Yeah. It was probably bugged. How else would he have known about what transpired with Harrison? She'd take the car as far out of the city as she could, before trading it for another vehicle, something cheap to take her wherever she decided to go.

Dressed in black, hoodie on her head, dark sunglasses covering her eyes, Sapphire parked the Spyder in view of the library. She arrived early, hoping to catch a glimpse of Harrison before he saw her.

He arrived promptly at six o' clock.

She smiled. He looked, so handsome...clean-shaven, his wavy hair freshly cut. He was casually dressed in a crisp button down shirt, dark colored vest, and jeans. He carried a bouquet of flowers, and to her surprise, the boy was with him. They sat on the stairs, the child beside him, elbows on his knees, hands resting against his plump cheeks. Harrison, to her eyes looked so hopeful, despite everything he'd been through with his wife. He looked to the future, and here she was, still trapped in the past. Victor was right. Harrison deserved better, so much better than what Sapphire knew herself able to offer.

Harrison and his kid stayed an hour and a half, the two of them watching pedestrians walk by, wondering if she would eventually show up. And he might have stayed longer, if a mist of rain hadn't begun to pour down. She wanted to reach out, to tell him how she felt, what she wanted, but knew that she shouldn't.

He gathered the boy up into his arms, shielding him from the rain as he dumped the flowers in a nearby trashcan before walking away. Though not before a lingering glance at the library, still, a measure of hope that Sapphire just might appear.

"I'll see you again, someday…" she said, muttering a quiet goodbye.

Sapphire watched until she could no longer see them, before driving off, destination unknown. Maybe, just maybe she could leave the past where it belonged. But she'd made too many powerful enemies for that, and there were still those who still deserved a proper comeuppance. No, as much as she wanted her life of espionage to end, she wasn't done yet. Not by a long shot…. The END

Sapphire's journey and romance with Victor
Reid begins in the prequel,
Sixth Iteration by E. Hughes

Available at via fine retailers everywhere.

For questions or comments
reach out to the author via the website:
http://ehughesbooks.com

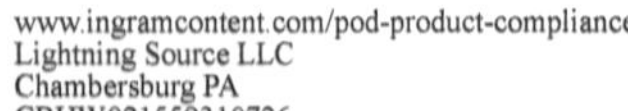